Believing in Myself!

Written by
Erica Pullen

Illustrated by
Kerry G. Johnson

Acknowledgments by the author, Erica Pullen

To my amazing mother, Joanne Haynes who never, ever gave
up on me despite my insecurities with my dark skin, and to
my wonderful husband, Wesley Pullen who is my biggest fan!
I love you both and truly thank you for *"Believing In Me!"*

Believing In Myself!

Text copyright © 2018 - Erica Pullen

Cover art, book design and illustration copyright © 2018 - Kerry G. Johnson

For permission requests, write to these email addresses
Erica Pullen: erical.pullen@gmail.com
Kerry G. Johnson: caricaturesbykerry@gmail.com

Published by TawKerr Publishing
A division of KGJ Design and Illustration

ISBN-10: 198524019X
ISBN-13: 978-1985240193

Printed in the United States of America

4

I keep trying and trying,
but I never seem to make it.

Seems my best is never good enough.

Well, I thought for sure
this would be my day.

I studied.

I practiced.

Wow, I thought for sure I would make it.

I was sitting on top of the world!

My blood was flowing and heart was pumping ...

... and for what?

They do what they always do,
they picked the pretty girls,
with long hair and pretty eyes.

Wow, those girls weren't even good, they were just cute!

12

Why is it that
I can never get
selected for
anything?

13

What about
freckled faced girls?

What about girls
with short hair?

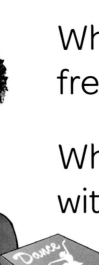

We're smart.

We're talented.

And we can sing
and dance ...

... just like the rest
of the girls!

Do you know what?

I'm going to start thinking positive
and follow my own dreams.

If no one else believes in me,
I will believe in myself!

Someday, other girls
and I will get picked
regardless of our
dark skin and kinky
hair or freckled face,
or even girls who
don't have long hair.

Someone out there will consider us "pretty"!

17

God made no mistakes
when he created me!

So look out,
Beyonce, Taylor Swift
and Kim Kardashian,
because here comes...

_____

insert your name

Believing in Myself!

Believing in Myself!

JOURNAL

Believing in Myself!
J O U R N A L

Believing in Myself!
JOURNAL

_____

_____

_____

_____

_____

_____

_____

_____

_____

_____

_____

_____

_____

_____

Believing in Myself!
J O U R N A L

Believing in Myself!
J O U R N A L

Believing in Myself!
J O U R N A L

Made in the USA
Lexington, KY
24 September 2019